Sire

An
Urban Romance

1
Sire

"Hey, Ms. Walker," I said, carving a couple slices from the hunk of roast beef in front of me. "Is Jalen going to make it home for the holidays this year?"

"No, hunny," she replied. "That boy said he don't have no leave this year. Ask me, I think he's gonna be laid up with some bobble head."

I couldn't help but laugh. Ms. Walker had always been a trip. Her son Jalen and I grew up together. From little league baseball, pop warner football, and even AAU basketball she'd been there to cheer her son on. And to say cheer is to put it mildly. Every time Jalen scored or made any kind of a play, you could hear Ms. Walker over every other person in the gym, and when a ref made a bad call she would be the first to storm the court, making sure that her point got across.

I know the refs wanted to hang their heads whenever they saw Ms. Walker coming.

All of that helicopter parenting must have been worth something, considering Jalen had been in the army for over a decade while I was still in the hood.

But, let's be real here. Even though I was still in the hood I wasn't hurting. Our paths to success had just been different. He chose to become a law abiding citizen, and I chose to become the King of the Streets. He chose to earn a paycheck and I chose to out-hustle everybody, embrace the violence and sliminess of our environment, and take what I want.

His idea of success was to get away from everybody we knew and start a new life with new people. My idea of success was doing exactly what I'm doing right now, giving back to my community, seeing faces that I've known my entire life as they stare back with a combination of admiration and envy because I *can* give back to the community.

"Tell you what," I said. "I'm going to have Thanksgiving dinner at my house. Nothing special or anything, just good food and a few friends. You should come through."

"Oh, no." She waved a hand my way. "I'll be fine. A few of us old ladies are gonna get together."

"At least let me bring you some pecan pie," I said as a huge smile crossed her face.

"Boy, you show up with some pecan pie, that's like showing up with an engagement ring. You might not be able to get rid of me so easily."

Yeah, she's a trip.

The community center was starting to fill up. We did this every year on the Saturday before Thanksgiving. I had a team of cooks in the kitchen putting in that work while I manned the serving lines. We also had a team of people on duty to clean up when each person was done with their meal.

Especially this year with the pandemic. We've all been so focused on social distancing and isolating ourselves from people that everyone was dying to congregate and share a few moments with others. I also understood the need for safety, so I threw in a bonus to anybody that would step up and take on sanitation duty.

This was just one of the ways I try to give back to the community that I've taken so much from. This is where every dime of my wealth came from. I've sold drugs, taken lives and possessions. I've robbed and killed. Whatever I had to do. All to build this empire. Literally everything I own came from these streets.

So these community events are akin to paying tithes and penance for me. Lord knows I owe my weight in gold.

As I continued cutting slices from the chunk of meat and setting them on plates, I felt a hand on my shoulder from behind, then a voice whispered into my ear, "Shipment got popped. Lay Low got away, but the laws got Dante."

My mood immediately tanked. What happened? How did the police get my shipment? Was it something Lay Low and Dante did on the road? Or, had the authorities been onto them the entire trip?

Too many questions and I knew the present would yield no answers, so I might as well put it out of my mind and focus on the task at hand.

Looking up, I saw a young boy staring at me. He couldn't have been older than ten. Shoving concern for my business and crew to the side, I gave him an extra thick slice of roast.

More penance, I guess. Things should get hectic in the weeks to come.

I'd known Dante for years and had a fairly favorable impression of him. But, he'd never done any time before. Neither had I, but we weren't cut from the same cloth. Dante was kinda soft. Like, he would fight... If he had to. And that fight would probably be over some chick he'd gone soft for that wasn't worth her weight in sand. After he'd cried a river over the fact that she'd just sucked the homie's dick and didn't care if Dante or anyone else knew about it because she wasn't relationship material to begin with.

As I thought about it I was surprised Dante was even in this game. But, greed and ambition can take a person out of their comfort zone, especially in a high value business like crime. You get so much return for the small amount of energy you put into it that nothing really compares. So a lot of people see the drug game as an industry in which you can be lazy and still reap the benefits of someone who makes over six figures a year.

Until the shit gets real.

How many times have you seen the most tightly run organizations get brought down because one person got jammed up and couldn't handle the time? I've seen it more times than I can remember. And no matter how

I try to mitigate the risk of my guys getting locked up, it happens.

Looking around behind the service line I spot Andrea, a drop dead sexy woman who had been working with me for a few years. We'd messed around a few times, but even as sexy as she was, Andrea didn't make me think of romantic walks down narrow Roman streets as we marveled at the history and art scattered throughout the city. She was solid people, though.

Catching Andrea's eye, I nodded my head for her to come and fill in for me. She knew how it was. I was the King, and I had affairs to keep in order. I'm sure she'd already heard about Dante and the shipment. News and rumors spread like wildfire and I'd obviously need to go handle the situation.

She approached as I untied my apron and handed it to her. Then I hustled out of the rec center's back door, grabbing my jacket in the process, and into my car, a black '67 Camaro with silver racing stripes on the hood.

My destination wasn't far, just around the corner and I made it there in no time. After parking, I walked past the main entrance of Patties, a burger joint that I co-owned with my cousin Mark, and approached a side entrance that led to a stairwell. Taking the stairs two at a time, I used a key to open the door at the top and walked into a large, open space that ran the area of the restaurant below.

This was HQ. Almost every decision involving my organization was discussed and finalized in this office.

I sat at my desk and looked over to the bank of monitors that rested to my side on the short end of my L-shaped, mahogany desk. These monitors were linked to various security cameras within my area of operations. Looking at the first two tiles on the top left of the screen I could see what's directly in front of the two doors that I'd just come through. Every angle on the outside of this building was covered, as well as the inside of Patties.

Three guys were approaching the outside door and I followed their progress until they reached the door at the top of the stairs. I pressed a button beneath my desk that unlocked the door with a buzzing sound and watched as the guys first heard the buzz then reached for the door to open it.

"Sire," said the first man through the door. It was the voice that had whispered to me in the center. He gestured for the second man to come in. "We knew you'd want to talk to Lay Low."

"Thanks, Menace," I said, then directed my attention toward Lay Low.

He was obviously nervous, as he repeatedly ran his hand over his short, wavy hair. But, why?

"Tell me what happened," I said to Lay Low.

"Man, I don't know," Lay Low said. "We just pulled up to a stoplight and then cars just started blocking us in from every direction."

I questioned, "So how did you get away?"

"Dante was driving, so when I saw all of the cars start to block us in, I hopped out and took off running. I thought Dante was gonna jump out too."

"Take off your clothes," I directed.

"Wh-what?" Lay Low stammered.

I gave Menace a slight nod of the head.

Menace's fist connected with Lay Low's jaw, dropping him to the floor.

"Get up," I commanded, rising from my seat. "I'm going to tell you one more time. Take off your fucking clothes. Right the fuck now."

"Look, Sire," he pleaded as I stepped around my desk. "I didn't do nothing. Please, man. Don't-"

I sent a heavy punch into Lay Low's stomach, causing him to double over as I grabbed his shirt and ripped it from his back.

"You wearing a wire? You working for the feds?"

"Naw, Sire. I'd never."

"Strip nigga. I don't know what the fuck you think this is, but being a narc is unacceptable. Now strip before I kill your bitch ass."

Removing what remained of his tattered shirt, Lay Low did as commanded and stripped naked. Fear and confusion coated his face like wax on a fresh paint job. He held a hand in front of his shriveled penis as he shifted his weight from foot to foot.

Bean, the third person to come through the door with Menace and Lay Low, gathered the discarded pile of clothes that had been dropped on the floor, and after crossing the room to a window, he threw the clothes out and watched them dance lazily through the air until they landed on the asphalt of the delivery area out back.

"Tell me what happened again," I said to Lay Low.

He went through the story for the second time. The same story, no deviation. The only difference was that his nakedness made him extremely uncomfortable and he spoke with a stutter.

I believed him. I didn't take him for a snitch, but I had to be sure. If law enforcement was picking off my shipments then there had to be a line of information traveling their way.

"Get the fuck out of my office."

"But, I don't have any clothes."

"I don't give a fuck. You ran and left your homie behind. We're a team and you can't even tell me what happened to him. Ol' scary ass nigga. Get the fuck outta my office!"

He looked unsure for a moment, taking half a step toward the door then turning back like he had something else to say. The look on my face left no room for questions or comments and after a couple shuffles back and forth he walked out of the door, cupping his dick in his hands.

After the door closed, Bean burst out laughing.

"Yo! You see how scared that nigga was? I'm surprised he didn't piss himself right in the middle of the floor!" Bean said through the laughter.

"Straight up," Menace responded. "But, if he ain't the rat then we have a real problem on our hands."

"Facts," I agreed. "I'm going to have Trent sweep all of our spots for bugs."

Bean said, "I don't trust them muthafuckas at Central Security. I know they be working with the laws."

"I don't, either," I said. "But I do trust Trent. Let everybody know he'll be coming by."

My mind shifted back to Dante and the fact that I didn't trust him, either. Maybe a little insurance policy could go a long way toward establishing the confidence I needed.

2
Daygo

Grabbing a handful of her thick, curly hair, I pushed her head down as hard as I could, forcing her to take as much of my dick as possible down her throat until she gagged and fought for air. That shit felt good as fuck, so I made her take it until she tapped out on my leg in an earnest attempt to breathe. Then I released her head, and she took a couple deep breaths.

In. Out.

In. Out.

She smiled.

Taking the tip between her lips, she tried to drain me, but I wasn't ready to let her have my cum, yet.

The ringtone blared from my phone, momentarily distracting my mind from the tongue swirling around my dick. Glancing at the screen I saw that it was the homie, Gotti. Whatever he had going on could wait, and I focused my attention back to the magic this chick was working on my dick.

Seriously. If there was a dick sucking Olympics she would be the gold medalist in marathon deep throating.

I grabbed a handful of her hair and pulled it back so that her face was looking up at the ceiling, tongue out. Slapping my dick on her tongue a few times, I let myself ride the rough surface back until I felt resistance as the head tried to enter her throat.

"Shit," I moaned. "Fuck."

Gripping the back of her neck, I fucked her pretty, caramel hued face as her gag reflex made my knees weak every time my dick went deep.

The fucking phone yanked at my attention again, it's shrill ringtone like nails on a chalkboard, and I forced my rock hard dick into the paradise that was her throat as I snatched my phone from the bed.

"Where's the fucking fire?" I answered.

"You need to get to the spot," Gotti said.

"I'm busy," I said as her hands began beating against my legs. She was fighting for air and that gag reflex was going crazy. "Fuck. Hold on."

I threw the phone down just as the spasms took me. My dick contracted, shooting cum down her throat. I released the hold on her neck and she drew back, taking heaving breaths as I sprayed the rest of my seed across her face.

Picking the phone back up, I said, "What's up?"

"They hit that shipment. We need to start planning our next move."

"I'm on my way," I said.

After pulling my pants up, I dug a couple hundreds from my pocket and threw them on the bed.

"Keep that shit wet," I said, walking out of the door. "I'll be back later."

Walking out of the apartment, the bright sun caused me to squint as I threaded through the buildings on my way out of the complex. After crossing through the wrought iron gate I walked a couple blocks to the corner store where I bought some blunt wraps and a candy bar. The spot was just around the corner and the candy bar would recharge the batteries that had just been drained by... I didn't even know

16

her name. She was just some new little thang that had moved into the hood a few weeks ago. Everybody had been trying to holla at her, but all these bitches hear is money talking. So I let Benjamin have a few words with her and the next thing you knew, my dick was in her stomach.

A throat with that kind of talent was worth the two hundred I'd left behind and I was thinking of giving her a recurring role.

The spot was a house, three doors down from the corner, and as I turned onto the quiet street I pushed her out of my mind to focus on our next moves.

Walking in, I was met by a pungently sweet aroma emanating from a bowl filled with frosty, light green buds resting on a scarred coffee table in the middle of the front room. I closed my eyes and took a deep breath. Nothing smells better than fresh, quality weed. I don't fuck with that hay smelling shit.

"Yo!" I called out to the empty room. "Where everybody at?"

I sat on the couch, coffee table in front of me and pulled the wraps from my pocket. After rolling up, I lit the tree and hit it deeply. The flavors of pineapple and pine washed over my mouth as the smoke filled my lungs to their maximum capacity, throwing me into a coughing fit.

Gas.

A couple hits later, Gotti and Byrd walked in the front door and I said, "Where the fuck y'all been? Calling me like the world was about to end, then when I get here you niggas ain't nowhere to be found!"

Gotti said, "I see you found the weed."

"Damn right."

"Pass that shit," Byrd said.

I hit it one more time then passed it to Byrd as he took a seat on the couch next to me.

"So, talk to me. What happened," I prompted Gotti since he was the one that had been blowing me up.

Gotti grabbed the blunt from Byrd and said, "We called in the truck, just like you told us to, and followed-"

Interrupting him, I said, "They didn't see you, did they?"

"Nah," Gotti paced as he spoke. "We had already scoped the route, remember? So we just had to make sure they was moving, then we fell all the way back and just cruised the route to see if anything was going down."

"Yeah, we saw a group of bad bitches, too," Byrd said. "I'm talking 'bout asses fat as fuck."

Gotti smiled, then continued. "Since we was staying back we missed the jump off, but the passenger door was wide open like the passenger took off running, and they had the driver on the ground while they searched the truck."

"They definitely found the dope?" I asked.

"Yeah, they did. But don't this make us snitches now?" Byrd asked.

"Snitching is a matter of loyalty," I said. "If we in some shit together and you get scared when the shit hits the fan and you give me up – that's snitching. This is… Using the tools available to us. We don't fuck with them niggas. Don't owe them shit. We just sewed a lot of confusion in their organization. They don't know who gave them up and while they're concerned with flushing out a rat, we hit them."

"That's bullshit," Gotti responded, arms spread wide. "Snitching is snitching. We all know what we're doing. We just gotta be comfortable doing it. If we pull this off we'll be set for a while. I won't have to do a bunch of hot, small time shit to keep my bills paid and my babies fed. The means are worthy of a bullet in our heads, but this time the end justifies the means."

"But we gotta be solid within this circle," I said. "If we doing this, we're doing it. In for a penny, in for a pound. You can still back out right now if you're uncomfortable with what we're doing. After this conversation is over I don't want to hear any more about it. You're either gonna get this money with me or not."

Gotti said, "I'm in. I know what the fuck is going on. Fuck them niggas. I got kids and I'm gonna make sure they have everything they need, no matter what I have to do. That nigga Sire and all them Hit Team niggas is sitting on a ton of dope and money. I'm coming for that shit."

"Byrd?" I asked. "You in or out?"

"I'm in. I need the money too."

"That's what's up," I said. "So, this is what we're going to do. They're probably gonna change up their shipping routes so we're gonna have to follow them and get their new movements. They'll be looking for the police to be on their tails, so be careful."

"Think they're going to switch up their schedule?" Byrd asked. "I don't want to be sitting out there all day waiting on a shipment that ain't coming."

Gotti looked at me and asked, "You're still fucking with Esmeralda, right?"

"Yeah," I responded. "I'm gonna stay over at her apartment for the next couple days so I can keep an eye on their stash house. I'll get all of their departure times and try to figure out if they're running any decoys and which vehicles they're using. I'll get pics, too. Y'all be ready to go when I get the info. And use different smoker buckets this time. We don't want them seeing the same cars over and over."

"I got you," Gotti said. "We're not gonna fuck this up. This is the biggest lick we've pulled and I'm counting on it going as smooth as silk."

To Byrd I said, "Get me a baggy. I'm taking some of this tree with me. This shit is some heat."

"Ain't it!" Byrd said, walking to the kitchen. "I met this chick and her brother grows for the dispensaries. She fucked around and took me by his house the other day and I slid back through that night and got his ass for a couple pounds of this shit."

After Byrd gave the baggie to me, I scooped up a handful of buds and dropped them inside. After pocketing the baggie, I stood and started for the door. "I'm headed to Esmeralda's. I'll get with y'all when I have what we need."

Heading out on foot, I turned in the direction of my mom's house, where I keep my car parked. As long as I'm in the hood I prefer to travel by foot. Don't have to worry about getting pulled over for a broken tail light or a forgotten turn signal. If someone starts shooting I won't be trapped like a crab in a steel and fiberglass barrel, and I can run in any direction if need be. Never know. Police could pull up at any moment and the freedom to run could be a life saver.

The route to my mom's house took me past the corner store where a group of guys stood off to the side of the building.

"Daygo," one of the guys yelled as I walked past. "Where your freaky ass momma at?"

Another guy chimed in, "We had her at the trap the other night, stripping. Bitch got so drunk she was dancing on the coffee table and pissed all over it before slipping in her own piss and falling off the table. Shit was hilarious! Lil Dre bout shot her ass for that shit."

A round of laughter circled through the group as the fire burning in my gut spread throughout my body. "Fuck you," I mumbled.

"What you say, lil nigga?" called the guy who had first said something to me, as his homeboys stood tall around him.

That's why I be robbing these niggas. I never had a choice when it came to whom I was born. It wasn't my fault that my mom was familiar with a lot of guys around the hood, but nobody would let me ignore or forget it. Shit was funny to them. Some kind of fucking joke.

One time I'd even tried talking to my mom about her reputation around the hood and the way everybody would throw it up in my face. Her response was to stay out of her business and that she was a grown ass woman and could do what she wanted.

I was alone and he had his guys with him, so this wasn't the time for confrontation. "Nothing," I said, the whole time thinking about how I was going to creep by his house tonight.

The door to the store opened and my mood immediately brightened. Three chicks had walked out and my attention was immediately drawn to Maia, this fine ass, honey hued piece that I'd had a thing for since middle school, even though she was a couple grades ahead of me. She still saw me as that little kid, so every time I tried to talk to her she shot me down.

That was ok, though. She'd come around once I got my money up and she could finally see that I was now a man. Until then, the sight of her fine ass would have to do.

3
Maia

"Gurl, these niggas is out here paying," CoCo was saying as we stepped off the bus to the sidewalk below. "School is cool and all, but it don't pay bills and these bills gotta get paid."

I loved my girls to death, both CoCo and Shay, but they could be a little much at times. I understood that the advice they were giving me was practical and spot on, but I just couldn't bring myself to lay up under some man just to keep the lights on. I mean, what happened to love and building relationships that would last a lifetime? The stuff that my grandparents shared? I guess true love that lasts a lifetime had been replaced with good sex that brought you eighteen years of baby daddy drama.

Not for me. It was looking like my nephew and I would get a good night's rest without electricity distracting us from dreamland. Especially since my no good brother got locked up before giving me his part of the rent money, leaving us in this situation.

I was in class when the call came in, and I recognized the county jail's number as soon as I looked at the screen. The teacher was going over a diagram of the central nervous system, a very important thing to know since I was training to be a nurse. It would also come in handy if I ever decided to become a serial killer, which was how I was feeling at the moment, knowing the lights were going to be cut off and there wasn't a damned thing I could do about it.

"I'm just not like that," I said.

"What?" Shay questioned. "A hoe?"

"Yeah, bitch. A hoe."

"Shit, you mean I get to bust a nut and get paid? Count me in." Shay cupped her breasts and arraigned them ever so perfectly, then let her hands slide down the sides of her curvy, goddess-like body to her hips, slapping the side of her ass for punctuation.

A group of guys on the side of the corner store saw Shay's display and issued a few whistles and catcalls in response.

"Not them, though," CoCo said. "They broke. My girl, Layla, used to fuck with one of them niggas and let me tell you, he was a no job having, part time hustling, bum ass nigga that blows all of his nickel and dime ass money smoking that water with all his other bum ass homeboys. She said he couldn't even get it up most of the time. I told her to get a Massage Master 3000 and forget about him."

"Massage Master 3000?" I questioned, raising an eyebrow.

"Bitch, you betta get you one," CoCo responded.

"I'm not interested," I shot back. "In your Massage Master, or them dudes."

"You'll never need a man again. Except for when it comes time to pay them bills."

We entered the store amid our own laughter and stares from the guys hanging out in front. A couple of them were cute, but they didn't have anything better to do than hang outside the corner store all day and that was a major turn off. A man is supposed to have some business to handle, something to do. If you can hang out at the store all day then you have too much idle time on your hands, and we all know that's the devil's playground.

As I browsed the cooler for something to drink I had to admit that the thought of having someone to help when times got tough has crossed my mind. I didn't plan on being some spinster aunt, raising my nephew and never having a family of my own. I just didn't get excited by any of the prospects I saw on a daily basis. There were some cool guys around, but the depth of their conversation wasn't much beyond that of a kiddie pool and you had to have more than just swag and a big dick to hold my interest.

Coke in hand, we left the store and the sun made me squint my eyes as a voice from behind called out, "What's up, Maia?"

I turned toward the familiar voice of a lean, light-skinned guy who'd always had a crush on me. He wasn't unattractive or anything, just young with an odd energy about himself. He'd always been polite and pleasant when it came to me, but still... You know how you just get a certain feeling about some people? I wasn't interested but I didn't want to hurt his feelings either. Just something in my gut.

The smile I offered was one a big sister would give a little brother as I said, "Oh, hi. Why you not in school?"

A look crossed his face that was part confusion, part disappointment.

"School?" he responded, voice raised an octave higher than normal. "I ain't been to school in a couple years."

"Oh," was all I could say, as an awkward silence settled over us.

Until CoCo's voice cut through the quiet as she said, "You're kinda cute. What's your name?"

His attention turned to CoCo as his gaze swept from her black, open toe boots, up her red leggings and black, form fitting sweater to the smooth, earthy brown skin of her face, finally meeting her eyes.

"I'm Daygo," he said in a confident tone that underlined the transformation that had occurred in the second it had taken him to turn from me to CoCo. Every time he'd ever talked to me it was with a slight quaver in his voice, as if he were slightly nervous. "I know who you are. CoCo, right? You used to dance up at The Red Light District."

CoCo asked, "You've been there before?"

"Yeah, but it's been a few months. Been kinda busy lately."

Holding a hand out, CoCo said, "Let me see your phone."

After digging in his pocket, Daygo came out with a phone and unlocked the screen, giving it to her.

After tapping on the screen for a moment she gave the phone back and said, "Call me and maybe we can set up a private show."

CoCo gave me a wink as she turned back around. We walked off, disappearing around the corner as Daygo stood and watched us go.

"You didn't have to give him your number. I had it," I said.

"Please. I didn't give him my number. He's gonna be in for a real surprise because the CoCo on the other end of that line can't quite figure out if she's a man or a woman."

Covering my mouth, I said, "Noooo! You didn't!"

"Mm hmm. Don't be surprised if his voice is a little higher the next time you see him," she said as a mischievous smile tugged at her full lips.

That girl was just too much at times.

Our little trio stayed together for a couple more blocks before breaking off to go our separate ways. Really, it was me who had to go the separate way since CoCo and Shay stayed a few doors down from each other. My place was a walk-up apartment in a building of six such dwellings a few blocks in the opposite direction, all accessed through a single front door with a column of buzzers to the side for visitors.

Overlooking the buzzers, I stuck my key into the lock and walked up two flights of stairs to my third floor abode. There were two apartments on each floor, and as I approached my door I reveled in how quiet and peaceful this place was. Outside of my nephew, only one other family in the building had kids, but they were exceptionally well behaved and the other residents were middle aged and over. When I had first applied for this apartment the owner wasn't enthusiastic about renting to someone as young as I, but after a couple conversations I was able to convince him that I wouldn't ruin the ambiance or the actual property itself, and he gave me the lease.

As I slid the key into my apartment's lock the door pushed open, already unlocked and ajar. My heart rate kicked up for a couple beats until I thought of my nephew. He was only ten and on break from school for Thanksgiving. Must have opened the door for some odd reason and forgot to secure it. He was young and the responsibility gene probably hadn't activated yet. I would talk to him and explain the importance of security. I'd worked too hard to acquire the few things that I owned and was in no rush to invite someone in to steal my stuff.

The short hallway just inside the door offered a brief hint of an unfamiliar scent, but I didn't give it much thought as I dropped my keys into a bowl on top of the small hallway table. Not wanting to call out my nephew's name in case he was sleeping, I first looked in the living room then moved on to the hall leading to the apartment's two bedrooms, the hardwood floor giving a small squeal of protest as I marched toward his bedroom door.

I could see that the door was open but my angle prevented me from getting a look inside. Once the interior of the room came into view I saw my nephew sitting on his bed with a suitcase next to him. A pile of clothes and toys were nearby awaiting their turn to be thrown into the luggage.

He looked like he was preparing for a vacation.

"Chris," I said in a soft voice as I crossed into the room. "Chris, hunny. What are you doing?"

"He told me to pack my stuff," Chris replied.

I was thinking that Chris was talking about an imaginary friend. Had to be. But I asked, "Who?"

Not saying anything, Chris extended a finger toward the closet. Turning my head in the direction he was pointing, I released a brief scream. Brief only because the man standing in front of Chris's closet took two long strides and clamped a hand over my mouth as soon as the scream escaped my lips.

"I'm not going to hurt you or the boy," he said as I stared up into his determined, brown eyes. "You have my word. Now, I need you to give me your word that if I take my hand from your mouth you won't scream again. Do I have your word?"

I tried to say yes, but the words came out as a muffled mess.

"Just nod your head." His voice was calm and deep, measured but edgy.

I nodded, and when he removed his hand I could still feel the strength of his touch on my lips as I started to ask a question, but had to clear my throat in order to get it out. My heart rate was going crazy and my stomach was in knots. "Who are you? Why are you here?"

"Lil Man is coming to stay with me for a while," he responded.

"I don't even know who you are! Chris isn't going anywhere!" I turned to Chris. "Baby, put your stuff back up for me."

"Nah, he's coming with me. It is what it is. I'd very much appreciate it if you helped me get his things together, though."

The knots that I now recognized as fear gave way to a burning anger as I said, "Just who the hell do you think you are?!? Marching up in here like you're running something. You better get up out of here before I call the police and have your ass all over the news for an amber alert."

He smiled.

He actually smiled.

The nerve! The audacity!

"I think we started out on the wrong foot. Look, nobody is going to call the police. Hell, fucking with the police is what got us here to begin with-"

"Are you with Child Protective Services, or something?" I interrupted.

"No. I'm Sire."

"What's that supposed to mean?" I shot back.

"You have interesting eyes," he said, causing me to look into his.

His gaze was intense but I felt no hostility. Just the opposite, in fact. I felt a warmth emanating from his eyes, and for a brief moment I felt a sense of safety.

Until I remembered that there was a strange man in my apartment trying to take my nephew.

"You his mom?" he asked.

I shook my head. "He's my nephew."

"Never in a million years would I have pegged you for Dante's sister." His eyes traveled the length of my body. "Y'all don't look anything alike."

"So, this has something to do with my brother," I stated, trying to figure out what was going on.

He stared at the ceiling as if considering something. Then, decision made, looked directly at me. Into me. Through me. His gaze was penetrating and I suddenly felt exposed, undressed. I began fidgeting beneath his scrutiny, shuffling my weight from foot to foot.

"Dante's in jail and Lil Man is going to come stay with me until he gets out. He's gonna be well taken care of. He'll have the best of everything. It's just that Dante needs to know that he's with me so when it's the middle of the night and he's considering decisions about his future the fact that I have his son will play prominently into those decisions."

"You think my brother is going to rat you all out."

He said, "I'm going to make sure he doesn't."

"By kidnapping a ten year old boy!" I said, incredulous.

"Kidnapping implies that he's under threat of some kind of physical harm. He's not. He'll be safer than he's ever been with all the supervision, toys, and space to run around that he could want." Turning toward Chris, he said, "Ice cream, too."

Chris' face lit up at the mention of ice cream.

"I don't even know your name," I said.

"I already told you. I'm Sire."

"That's your name?"

Nodding his head, he asked, "And you?"

"Maia."

"Well, Maia… Mind helping me get his stuff together? I have a lot on my plate and I need to get this done so I can get back to it."

"I'm not letting you take Chris without me."

Sire said, "You weren't invited."

"He doesn't go if I don't go," I said, hands on my hips.

He smiled again, rows of straight, white teeth in contrast with his mahogany skin and dark, full beard. "Pack everything you can. Might be staying for a while."

4
Sire

The woman walking into the room presented an interesting problem and I stood in front of the closet running through different courses of action, all of which would have been effective at neutralizing the problem while creating a whole shit storm of other problems at the same time.

Thankfully, the need to execute any course of action wasn't necessary. I'm not sure if I was able to convince her that I meant them no harm, or if she could tell that I wasn't leaving this apartment without the boy. Whatever the case, I was relieved when she relented and even volunteered to come along with him.

Chris insisted on carrying his own bag out to the truck, determination written on his face as he hefted and heaved his suitcase around, but he made it. Maia ended up with two bags of her own, one of which I carried down wondering what the hell she had inside that caused it to be so heavy. Felt like a bag of rocks, but I didn't let on how heavy it was. I just carried the lead filled – or so I suspected – bag and lifted it into the back of the truck, hoping that my back didn't go out.

It wasn't actually that bad, but still, I had an itch to open it up.

Chris climbed into the back of the Quad Cab, then Maia and I hopped into the front and I started the truck.

Once I started driving, Maia asked, "This electric?"

"Pulled the engine and did the conversion myself."

"*You* did it?" she asked with more than a hint of skepticism in her voice.

"What? Gangstas can't be smart too?"

"I didn't say that." Maia shook her head. "So… What was my brother into?"

I responded, "He worked for me."

"Ok, so what are *you* into?"

"Profit," I replied. "Coke and ice, mostly. That's where your brother worked with me. I have a few legal business ventures too."

"How did he get locked up?" she asked, looking out of the window.

"I'm not really sure. We're looking into it now. All I know is that they were on the road, on their way to make a drop when they were boxed in at a light. The passenger jumped out and took off running, but Dante was driving and didn't get away."

"Who was he with? Can you trust him?"

"I think so," I said as I pulled to a stoplight and looked around, imagining being surrounded by a bunch of vehicles. "He was reprimanded for leaving Dante behind. We're a team. We don't leave any of our guys. We get money together, fight together. Ride or die together. I think he understands that now. Other than that he's always been pretty solid.

Maia tilted her head upward, then a moment later she said, "It was like I didn't even know my own brother these last few years. So many secrets. When we were kids we were close and told each other everything. It was just me and him most of the time. Then... I don't know. He got caught up in the streets and he changed. Stopped talking to me."

Not knowing how to respond to that, I said nothing. Sometimes people don't need a response, or an answer. Her tone suggested that she was thinking out loud more than anything else. She didn't strike me as being afraid to ask questions or say what's on her mind, so I just let it ride, giving my own thoughts space to organize themselves.

The question that kept tugging at me was how the authorities knew about my delivery.

Everybody knew their routes and schedules, so there wasn't a need to talk about it. Even though I was having every place we used swept for bugs, I really didn't think that was our problem. Bugs can't pick up what's not being talked about. For them to be boxed in like that at a stoplight was evidence that it wasn't something they did on the road. How would law enforcement be able to set up that type of response without my guys ever being aware of it if this was all over some traffic violation? The police would have hit the lights off top.

There was a piece to the puzzle missing and I wouldn't find the answers I was looking for until I figured out what that piece was.

Right now, I needed to reroute all of my transports. Might as well compartmentalize things as well. The only people who needed to know the route were the people driving it. The other teams didn't need to know any other teams' business, keeping them from giving up the goods on anyone but their own damn self. From my experience people weren't enthusiastic about telling on themselves.

After waiting for the gate to open and turning into my driveway, the truck climbed the steep rise until it leveled off then drove past my house, pulling into the detached three car garage in back. As we walked to the back door

I could see the gate rolling back into its secured position.

My house was the biggest on the block, a three level, five bedroom with white and smoke gray siding. When I'd first bought this house it was a piece of crap. The exterior was weathered and the paint had been almost completely eroded, exposing the bare wood. It had looked like something out of a scary movie. I didn't mind because it wasn't only the biggest house on the street, but was also the best deal in the housing market.

The back door opened to the kitchen. What had been saved on the actual purchase price of the house had been used renovating the interior. The kitchen was a cook's dream. It was spacious, with white soapstone counters and a black, white, and gray backsplash.

Sitting Maia's suitcase on the tiled kitchen floor, I said, "Leave your bags here and go upstairs and pick out your rooms. All the rooms on the second floor are empty, so you can use any one you like."

"The profit business must be good," Maia said, a hint of something I couldn't quite put my finger on in her voice.

"Sheets, towels and everything else you'll need should be in the hallway closet. Make yourself at home."

They disappeared up the stairs while I headed to my first floor office, pulling my phone from my pocket.

"Mark," I said once the line was answered. "What are you doing tonight? I need you to take a ride with me. Some shit's been going on and I need someone I can trust to help me figure a few things out."

"You know I got you, Sire. Just let me know when you're ready," Mark replied.

"I'll be there in about thirty."

Clicking off, I made another call and when it was answered, I said, "Andrea, I have Dante's lil boy and his sister at my house. I need you to come sit on them for a little bit."

"You want me to babysit?" she shot back.

"Just make sure they don't try to jet out the back door while I'm not around. As long as they're here Dante won't do any talking. If you gotta babysit to keep the team safe then that's what you'll do. I gotta go and map out new transportation routes. Think I wanna be doing this shit? Hell no, but it has to get done. You're up, so get your ass over here and handle this shit."

I hung up to her resigned, "Alright."

Ten minutes later I heard a car pull into the driveway and I got up to go out and meet Andrea. As I went out of the back door I noticed that the luggage had disappeared. Good. They must have found the rooms they wanted and were making themselves comfortable. Chris didn't say anything the whole ride over and I wondered how he would fare with this interruption to his daily life. Kids are resilient, but I'd do everything I could make his time under my roof as stress free as possible.

I smiled to myself thinking about stress and how at times I wished that I was a kid again. No bills, no responsibility. What could there be for a kid to stress about? I could understand why adults would want to be kids again, but for the life of me I couldn't understand why every kid wants to be an adult. The perceived freedom is just an illusion. We all serve some master.

Andrea looked good - as always - as she stepped from her baby blue BMW M8 in white and pink retro Jordans and painted-on jeans. Long box braids flowed down her curvy backside and I wondered how she could drive without sitting on her hair.

"You know I don't do kids, Sire. You owe me for this one."

I responded, "I know you were born without the mother gene. That's why Dante's sister is here. She'll watch the kid. You watch her."

42

Climbing into my Camaro, I drove to Patties where Mark was outside in the parking lot smoking a cigarette while he waited on me.

"Bout time," he said once I'd pulled into the lot.

"I had to wait on Andrea to come over."

Mark plopped his 6'3", two hundred and seventy pound frame down into the passenger seat and asked, "Y'all fucking around again?"

"Nah. I mean, don't get me wrong. It was good, but that was it. I need something deeper. Millions of women are fine with some good pussy. But experiencing those deep emotions... You know what I'm talking 'bout. Like what you and Zaria had. That shit is rare."

Mark raised his eyes to the sky, holding the gold cross that hung around his neck between thumb and forefinger. "Yeah, it is. And that damned cancer took her from me far too soon."

"Have you been dating?" I asked as I pulled out of Patties' parking lot into traffic.

"Here and there. Nothing special though. The crazy thing is that I keep comparing every woman I meet to Zaria. It's not fair to the women, but I can't help it."

"It's only been two years," I said. "I still compare women to girls I had crushes on back in middle school."

"Like Tasha." Mark said with a chuckle. "Boy, you had it bad for her. I remember you used to carry around that picture you drew of her in your backpack all day."

"And she would never even look my way." I smiled to myself. "A couple years ago she tried to throw it at me. Didn't even remember who I was. All she knew was that Sire was ringing bells in the streets."

"You smash?"

"Hell yeah! You think I wasn't? I'd been dreaming of this girl since I was eleven."

"What?!? I never knew that!"

"It was nothing. By then, I could see her for who she really was. Everybody with a name was fucking her."

Mark said, "Ah. She was looking for a come-up."

"A true bag chaser," I confirmed.

We rode in silence for a couple minutes, both of us traveling back in time on the wings of memories. The crushes of my youth had all turned out to be underwhelming in adulthood. I had to learn that youth, along with all of the hormones raging throughout a teenager's body, causes us to see through rose colored lenses as we deal with the opposite sex. There were a few girls that I had put on a pedestal back in the day, not really knowing them.

44

Growing up had peeled off the shiny exterior, revealing the bullshit beneath.

Or, at least, they just weren't for me.

Mark's gruff voice brought me back to the present. "I know you didn't call me for help with your love life, and I know for damn sure I don't want your help with mine. So, what's up? Why are we out cruising around lovely Duncanville tonight?"

"The police took down one of my transports. They had to know about it ahead of time. The route and everything. They were already set up, waiting on my guys. So now I don't know if someone is talking inside my organization, or what. You are the one person I know I can trust with absolute certainty. I have five distribution routes I need to rework, and you're gonna help me.

5
Daygo

I stood in the window of Esmeralda's apartment, waiting for movement out of the Hit Team's stash house. Alternating between sitting in an uncomfortable, wooden chair and standing, I had passed the night staring at nothing.

Nothing.

Not even a mouse could be seen moving around their stash house. WTF was going on? Did they switch up locations? Couldn't have. That would be a massive undertaking. They'd have to move all of the equipment necessary to run a large scale drug business. Two ways they could go about it. Move everything in one big ass truck that was obvious as fuck, but would only take one trip. Or use cars and either make a lot of trips back and forth or use a lot of cars at once.

I saw neither of those things happening. Looked like the place had been abandoned for the past few years.

So… They had deserted the stash house. I wondered if someone was nearby with an eye on the place to see who might come by. They wouldn't know who to trust right now and that could be one way to catch a dumb ass traitor. I knew it would be a waste of their time, but still.

Reaching for the ashtray, I plucked out the remnants of a blunt that I'd been smoking throughout the night. It had been put out a few times since it was that good tree that I'd taken from the spot and just a few hits were enough to have me lit.

I wondered, again, if we could just hit the stash house. My previous observations led me to believe that it would be impossible short of a suicide mission, and I wasn't with the kamikaze shit. But looking at the place right now all I could think about was how all of that money and dope was just sitting there, unsupervised.

Unless this was a ploy to draw out the rat. Play dead and let the vermin come out and fall right into the trap. There was just too big of a morsel sitting out there waiting on someone to try and snatch it.

Which was exactly why I was still watching. I wasn't gonna fall for the banana in the tailpipe and go out like Boo-Boo the fool. My plan was to hit them while they're in motion, at their most vulnerable. Not in a stash house where they could compile their forces into one army. Nah, I had to divide and conquer. I didn't need the entire stash house, anyway. One of their shipments would do me well and put a couple hundred thousand in my pockets.

"Come to bed, Papi. You've been up all night, sitting at this window like some star crossed lover waiting on your girl to come walking down the street," Esmeralda said from behind me.

Turning to face her, I wrapped one arm around her waist and pulled her into my body. "You're my girl," I said, planting kisses on her lips between words. "And my lover."

Kiss.

"And if I'm star crossed."

Kiss.

"It's because you sucked the soul outta me."

Kiss.

"Before I put your ass to sleep earlier."

She smiled seductively and said, "Was that before or after I glazed your beard like a Krispy Kreme doughnut?"

I smiled. "It was right before you came like seven times."

"Oh, my God, I couldn't stop cumming. I think the bed is still wet."

"And I think I want you to cum again," I said as I took a knee and ran my hands along

48

Esmeralda's thighs beneath the hem of the t-shirt she slept in. Her skin was bare underneath. No panties. No bra. Her pussy was shaved smooth and a hint of something wet and sticky coated my fingers as I slid them between her folds.

With her back against the window, I threw one of her legs over my shoulder and let my tongue trace her pussy lips. Her pussy was so fat I could grip her lips between my lips and that shit was so fucking sexy.

Spreading her with my hand, I let my tongue taste every centimeter of her pussy, looking for that magic spot that would send her over the edge. She was dripping wet and I shoved my tongue as deep as I possibly could inside her walls. A moan escaped her lips as her head rolled back and her hands gripped my head.

The water works began to flow and she drip, drip, dripped down my chin. She was sweet with a hint of salty and I drank her flavor like I was a desert wanderer who had finally found his oasis.

Her breaths came more rapidly as the volume of her moans increased. Her pussy grinded against my face and I could feel her getting closer to a flash flood level event, so I locked my arm around the leg draped over my shoulder and waited for the rapids.

The orgasm took her like an earthquake and the dam broke, freeing the waters that had been held back. Her nectar sprayed my face, coating me from crown to chin.

I raised her shirt as I stood and let it fall to the floor. Then I turned Esmeralda around, pressing her bare breasts against the window and took her from behind. She was so wet that I slipped inside her almost accidentally with barely a hint of resistance and my throbbing dick entered her drenched vagina until I tapped that back wall and could proceed no further.

Arching her back, she moved against me, her already heavy breathing now coming in ragged gasps. I took a handful of her hair and pulled, making Esmeralda arch her back even further as I took my other hand and wrapped it around her throat.

"Yes. Just like tha-" Cutting her off mid-word, the moan that escaped her lips came from the depths of her being and she immediately shook and contracted, pushing me out of her juice box with a spray of ejaculate.

I tapped the head of my dick against her clit until her orgasm passed and the torrential downpour stopped. Then I entered her again as a trail of vaginal secretion meandered down my legs.

Looking down at her body, I admired the curve of Esmeralda's hips and ass, her golden, sun-kissed skin. I grabbed her waist and pulled her into me, the soft flesh of her stomach against the coarse skin of my hands, and bit her neck to a seductive coo.

I lifted my eyes as a pair of headlights outside caught my attention. The headlights pulled to a stop in front of the stash house in what were the first signs of activity the entire night. The lights died, thrusting the scene below back into the cover of darkness, but the moon provided enough illumination to make out the forms of two people exiting the car.

Esmeralda must have sensed that my mind had become distracted because she reached back, grabbing a hold of my ass with both of her hands, and pulled me into her. "Harder," she said.

Turning her chin toward me, I kissed her deeply as I gave her pussy a workout. She moaned into my mouth and put her hand behind my neck. I moved her long, dark hair out of the way and kissed the back of her neck and spine.

A light came on in a ground floor room and every now and then I could see a thin shadow pass through the light, but something in the window prevented me from making out any

51

particulars, kind of like the frosted glass you see on the doors of offices, but I'd seen the outside of the windows in the daylight and they weren't frosted. I wondered what they used because it would come in handy on the windows at the spot.

"Mmm, Papi. You know how to work this pussy so good."

Offering Esmeralda a slap on the ass I said, "Whose pussy is this?"

"Yours."

"Yours, what?"

"Yours, Papi."

Pulling her hair again, I pushed deep and hard until I could go no further, raising her on to the tips of her toes. I held her like that, keeping pressure on that spot deep inside her as a low, rumbling growl escaped her lips.

An upstairs light came on, but it was on the side of the stash and I wasn't able to look into the window although the warm glow could be seen in the dark of the night. The thought occurred to me that the stash house would be a honey hole, maybe even worth the risk to hit it. Especially if they kept clear of the place for a couple more days as they had tonight. If I had the tools and equipment I could have hit the place and cleaned it out with so little activity going on.

Esmeralda's fingernails dug into the skin of my thighs, bringing me back to the work being done currently. Squeezing her full breasts I took a nipple between my fingers and pinched. She rewarded my action with another of her sweet moans. My other hand went to her clit and her knees went weak, but my dick held strong, catching her and supporting her weight until she could support herself. It took a moment because as soon as I took her weight a round of convulsions shook her body, but she soon recovered and started grinding back against me.

The upstairs light at the stash house went out, thrusting the side of the house back into darkness.

Taking my thumb, I eased the tip into her ass and moved it in circles. She bent forward, consenting to this new incursion as a whole string of sensual profanity issued from her lips.

"Shit, Papi. I want you in my ass. Fuck me in my ass."

The light on the bottom floor of the stash house died and a moment later the two figures walked out of the house heading to the car.

Pulling my dick out of Esmeralda, I yanked my pants up. "I'll be right back."

Buckling my belt as I ran for the door, I darted out into the hallway, forgetting to close the door behind me. I ran down the stairs and into the parking lot, digging my car keys from my pocket.

There wasn't much traffic tonight – hell, there wasn't any traffic – so it should be easy enough to catch up and find their car.

Pulling into the street I turned in the direction I'd seen the car go, but there were no signs of tail lights directly ahead of me. I came upon an intersection and slowed down, looking down the cross street for signs of vehicles. After looking carefully both ways without seeing anything I continued on to the next intersection in a hurry while trying to not miss anything. The next intersection gave me the same results as the last and I wondered if I had lost them.

The next intersection provided more of the same as I looked to my left, but as I turned to the right I noticed that the street angled downhill and curved to the left out of sight. Then a short flash of red caught my eye even further down the hill. I had only seen it for a moment, but I was willing to bet that the car I was looking for had just revealed itself.

Turning in the direction of the flash I sped along the curving downhill road in an attempt to make up ground. The angle combined with the dark night skewed my depth perception, but I figured they were a half mile ahead.

A few curves later the road leveled out both horizontally and vertically as the red glow from a set of tail lights came into view. I was lucky that this road hadn't had any turnoffs, but that would soon turn out to be something of a disadvantage. No intersections meant it wasn't likely that any other cars would be joining us, leaving me exposed as the only following vehicle.

Fuck it.

Nothing to do about it now other than just sit back, cruise, and play it cool.

6
Maia

The reality was finally starting to settle in that I was something of a prisoner as the woman first knocked, then opened the door to the bedroom I'd chosen for myself.

She had introduced herself last night but I didn't remember her name. Yesterday was a blur as I tried to get Chris and myself settled into our new living arrangements. He didn't seem to be too upset, but you could never tell with kids. Sometimes they can be exceptionally good at concealing the way they feel about things and I was laser focused on making sure he was alright.

Morning sunlight leaked into the window as she asked, "You hungry? I made pancakes, sausage and eggs for breakfast."

A yawn escaped my lips and I stretched. "What time is it?"

She leaned against the door jam. "A little after seven. I'll give you a minute to get yourself together."

I threw the covers off and sat up as she turned and left, closing the door behind her. My feet hit the floor and I padded down the hall to Chris' room and opened the door. He was curled beneath the covers, a light snore on his lips.

Satisfied that Chris was ok, I went to the bathroom and turned the shower on. At least the electricity was working and I didn't have to do all this in the dark.

Looking around the bathroom, I thought about how nice it must be to have a house like this, to not worry about bills and rent, and about people who were supposed to take care of their half of things, but don't.

Must be nice.

After getting dressed, I got Chris up and together, then headed downstairs to the kitchen where we sat at an island and ate. The woman rested against the sink looking like everything that I wasn't. It was seven something in the morning, and let me tell you, her makeup was on point. She wore a cute dress and heels, and her nails were done with an intricate design. I could see her being some baller's girl, maybe even Sire's.

A hot flush washed over me at that thought and I looked at myself sideways for it. True, Sire was a handsome man in a rugged sort of way with his beard and those strong hands, but I obviously wasn't the type of girl he'd go for. Probably why What's Her Name was here; watching over her man while the new meat was in the house. Plus, he had kidnapped a ten year old kid. And, me. What kind of man would do something like that? Definitely not the kind I needed in my life.

Swallowing a bite, I had to admit that she could cook. "These eggs are good."

"I use duck fat instead of butter."

Duck fat? I didn't think that I'd ever eaten a duck before. "Are you his wife?"

She raised an eyebrow. "Girl, no. That man is blind to the charms of women. Sire? Married? Please. And, why you asking? Don't get your pretty little feelings hurt, now."

Getting the impression that I'd struck a bit of a nerve, I felt a sense of relief all the same when she said he wasn't married. "Am I allowed to go outside?"

"I don't see no bars. As a matter of fact I'm about to go out and get a few things for Thanksgiving. Can you cook?" she asked.

I nodded. "How long will I be here?

She shrugged. "Until Dante gets out, I guess. I'm pretty sure you'll be here for Thanksgiving, and I could use an extra pair of hands with this food."

"I'll help."

"Good," she said. "I like to get out before the stores get too crowded. And I know you're not wearing that."

Looking down at my skirt and sweater, I said, "What's wrong with it?"

"You look like a jury member for the Salem Witch Trials. I know you gotta have something different you can throw on."

"This is how I dress," I said, maybe a little too defensively.

"Ok, ok. At least let's get you something for Thanksgiving dinner. Everybody gonna be on they shit that day."

I relented. "Alright."

When in Rome, right?

The grocery store was crowded even though we tried to beat the traffic, but it was two days before Thanksgiving and seemed like everyone had waited until the last minute to get their menu together, driving some people mad. Two women were even fighting over the last can of jellied cranberry sauce.

"Bitch, I was here first!" one of the women screamed.

"Nu-uh. We got here at the same time, now let it go!" the other argued.

They wrestled over the can, crashing into shelves and knocking items all over the floor as everyone around them pulled out their phones to live-stream the chaos. One of the women tripped over her flip flop and crashed to the floor amongst all of the detritus scattered about to the jeers of the onlookers. The lady left standing offered one final kick to her downed opponent then raised the can in victory.

The crowd quickly lost interest and dispersed.

She shook her head. "People done lost their damned minds."

We meandered through the store until finding the seafood department where she ordered a small mountain of jumbo shrimp and crab.

A confused look crossed my face. "Seafood for Thanksgiving?"

"We ain't no pilgrims. The white folks can have their turkey and stuffing. We made our own tradition and we also try to mix something new into the dinner each year." She pointed to the shellfish. "That's for the gumbo I'm making."

The store offered a few more items of interest before we made our way to check out. She bought Chris a candy bar at the register then we carried our bags to the car.

Next, we stopped at a burger joint. She let Chris order whatever he wanted and we all sat at a booth close to the register as the food was prepared. Once it had been delivered and Chris was lost in his bacon cheeseburger she led me out the front door with a nod to the man at the till. Walking around the side of the building we entered another door and climbed a set of stairs that led to another door that buzzed loudly as we approached.

There were about ten people in the room, Sire sitting behind a large desk with his feet kicked up and the rest randomly scattered around.

The room went silent and heads turned our way as we walked in. "What the fuck y'all looking at? As quiet as it got in here you'd think a bitch came in walking on water or something."

"Andrea always talking shit," said a voice from among the pack.

A light went off when the guy said her name. I was too embarrassed to admit that I'd forgotten it so all day I just hadn't called her anything.

Another voice piped up. "Who's your homegirl? See, you be hiding bitches from us. Introduce her."

Andrea sucked her teeth. "Nah Squish, bitches just run and hide whenever they see your ugly ass coming. That's why you be having to break these hoes off just to get a lil taste of something wet."

The muscles in the Swish's jaw worked as he swallowed his anger at Andrea calling him ugly, but he didn't respond. She must have some rank within this circle because even though the guys gave her a hard time she gave it back even harder and I could tell the guys had a line they wouldn't cross with her.

Squish turned toward me and I felt worms crawling all over my skin as he silently stared at me, undressing me with his eyes. I looked away for a moment, hoping my lack of eye contact would be his signal to find something else to stare at. But when I looked in his direction again his eyes hadn't moved one inch. Licking lips that were burned black and peeling, he nodded at me and I tasted bile in the back of my throat.

He was repulsive. It wasn't that his features were unattractive, but the way in which they were positioned on his face combined with the facial expressions he made, brought to mind an image of the old man from Family Guy with the walker, only young and black.

I turned toward Sire and saw that he, too, was staring at me. When our eyes met it was as if I'd been punched in the stomach, all the wind knocked out of me as the rest of the room disappeared, leaving only the two of us.

Andrea's voice cut through, bringing the surrounding commotion back into focus as I took a breath. "We need to get your girl here something to wear for Thanksgiving."

Sire looked me up and down. "What's wrong with her clothes?"

She said, "Nothing, if she's going to mass. Come on, Sire. You gotta admit she dresses a little like a nun."

A few chuckles could be heard around the room.

Sire looked my way, putting me on the spot. "What do you think?"

I looked down at my outfit, took a deep breath. When in Rome, right? "I like my clothes, but I'm open to doing something different."

Sire opened a drawer in his desk, reaching in and grabbing a stack of money held together by a thick rubber band. Extending his arm, money in hand, he said, "Get whatever you need, Maia."

Looking at the money being offered, I was unsure about what to do. Imagining someone giving that much money to me so nonchalantly was almost unrealistic. Tendrils of anxiety started to work their way through my body and

I realized that I was nervous about taking the dough. People don't just hand out cash like that. There had to be some kind of catch and I just wasn't seeing it.

Noticing my hesitation, Andrea stepped forward to relieve Sire of the money, but as she reached he pulled it back with a shake of the head.

"Maia, you good?" he asked.

I stood frozen in place, staring at the bills. "I can't."

Sire raised an eyebrow in question.

"That's too much. I can't take that."

A voice in the room said, "Damn, I ain't never seen a bitch turn down free money before."

Sire's eyes flashed. "Shut the fuck up, Will. Actually... Get out. Everybody. Get the fuck out."

I turned to leave as everyone else stood and made their way to the door.

"Not you, Maia. Stay."

Once everybody departed, leaving Sire and me alone, I suddenly felt like a shy schoolgirl, fidgeting like I was waiting to see the principal.

Sire asked, "My money not good enough for you?"

"It's not that," I said, looking down at my feet. "It's just so much money. I couldn't possibly take it."

Standing, he walked around his desk and stood in front of me, lifting my chin with a finger. "It's ok. Money comes, money goes and I have plenty enough. Take it. It's yours. No strings. Just get what you need."

I could feel an energy emanating from him, a current charging the air between us. And, again, as he stared at me I felt exposed. Not like he was undressing me with his eyes, but as if he were peering straight into my soul with a magnifying glass, searching for the real me, the me that was buried deep down in the honeycomb patchwork that contained the very essence of who I am.

"I'll tell you what. You can work for it, just like everybody else. I'm a man short with Dante locked up right now and I could really use an extra set of hands. It won't be like the work you're used to, but since you don't want to take my money you can earn it."

"I don't know…"

He sighed. "Look. Not to be an ass or anything, but you invited yourself. I came for the boy, and as you can see, he would have been well taken care of. But, no. You insisted on coming with him only to refuse my hospitality. Ok, fine. So, work for it. Or leave. I can drop you off right where I found you and you can go back to doing whatever it is you were doing before you walked into that room and saw me. I don't have time to sit here and beg you to accept any-damn-thing I'm offering. So what's it gonna be? You in or out?"

There was no way I was leaving Chris by himself, no matter what I had to do to stay and make sure that he was safe. I honestly didn't think he was in any immediate danger or anything, but as long as Chris was here, I'd be here.

I held my hand out to take the money from him. "I'm in."

Sire gave me the rubber band wrapped stack of bills. "Go do what you need to do. Just be ready this evening because you're up."

7
Sire

Mark lived in a two bedroom, single level brick house a few streets over from Patties. After pulling into the driveway behind his five year old Tahoe, I went to the front door and got a strong whiff of fresh tree. Looking all around for the source I even gave myself a pat down before giving up and knocking on the door.

He was expecting me so it only took a few seconds for Mark to answer.

"You lose some tree out here? That shit loud as fuck."

He looked confused for a second before the eureka moment struck. "Shit. You can smell that out here?"

I nodded. "What, you got a pound sitting on the coffee table or something?"

Mark stepped back, allowing me to step inside the house. "Nah. Let me show you something."

He led me through the kitchen and into a laundry room with a washer and two dryers.

Kneeling in front of one of the dryers, he opened the door and a bright light spilled out, filling the compact space.

The inside had been hollowed out, with all of the components necessary for circulating hot air and tumbling clothes removed and replaced by one intense ass light and three short, bushy plants. This was the origin of the smell.

I knelt before the dryer. "You know I can smell this shit outside? You don't have any ventilation or odor control. All it takes is one mail man with a bias against drugs and the laws are gonna be all up in here."

Mark stroked his goatee and exhaled. "So what do I need to do?"

I asked, "How much space do you have out back?"

"There's nothing back there but the grill and a couple chairs. You thinking 'bout planting this stuff out back?"

I smiled. "Not planting. Think there's enough room for a shipping container?"

"Maybe one of the short ones."

I thought for a moment. "I'm gonna build you a grow room for the backyard. It'll have sufficient ventilation and odor control. But the best part is that it's gonna run off solar so you won't have to worry about a spike in your electricity usage. You'll be able to grow year round, maintain the climate and won't have to worry about power outages."

Mark burst out laughing, doubling over. "I forget your ass went to school for engineering. Sounding like a clean energy commercial. Fucking nerd."

"Well, this nerd is going to require half of all future harvests if you keep talking shit."

"Now there's the shark I know and love."

I said, "Keep talking. Your grow room is going to come with a specially delivered ass whoopin. You ready to go?"

Mark drove his Tahoe, since he was the one doing the shopping, and I sat in the passenger seat listening to music. The traffic was light and I guess that's to be expected on the day before Thanksgiving.

I turned the music down. "You coming to dinner tomorrow?"

"Ain't no way I'm missing Andrea's gumbo. That's who you need to invest in. That girl can cook."

Shaking my head I said, "She just ain't cut for that shit."

Mark chuckled. "People will surprise you."

"If she was with it I'd back her, but I'd be afraid for the first person on her staff who pissed her off within arms reach of a butcher knife."

The light traffic was slowly getting heavier and soon we saw protesters in the streets.

He hit the brakes, slowing down as we came to a standstill, surrounded by protesters.

I asked, "You know what this is all about?"

Mark sighed. "There was another police shooting."

"Damn," I said, shaking my head. "This bullshit gotta stop. They're killing us fam."

"The news said he had a gun."

"*You* shoot somebody and say he had a gun. You'll be arrested, tried, and convicted before you take your next breath. How is it that ordinary citizens are held to a higher standard than a trained police force? Doesn't make any sense. These people go through training for threat detection and thinking logically through fear. You can't convince me that they should be getting away with this shit. Think about it. They're nothing more than a gang that's been sanctioned by the government so they get away with shit the average guy can't. It don't even matter what race somebody is, they're going down if they're not wearing blue."

Mark shook his head. "They scared of us, Sire. Don't act like you don't know. You was one of the main ones bathing the city in blood back in the day. The police wouldn't even come into the hood without backup. And it wasn't just you. The whole set was piling up bodies. Of course they're gonna be on edge when they come through the hood. The tactics that they're learning today were put in place to deal with y'all bad asses!"

I didn't have an argument for that so I looked around at the faces of protesters and realized just how many people out here bringing attention to the black life lost weren't black. There were just as many other races as there were black faces. The diversity lightened my heart, because despite our differences we're more alike than unalike and change would only come with a greater understanding of that fact.

Mark's voice broke into my thoughts. "I never understood it. You were always too smart for the streets. You could have done anything you wanted. Why do this?"

When I was away at school I was something of a spectacle. Everybody looked at me like, *wow this is one of the guys from the music videos, but in real life.*

Did I try to fit in? Maybe not as hard as I could have, but I never thought it necessary to be anyone other than who I was. I love my hair. I love the way I dress. I love my swag. My culture is just as relevant as any other and I shouldn't have to shed it just to be successful.

To Mark, I simply said, "I found my tribe."

Turning the music back up, I let it drown out the voices of protesters, honking horns, and the cacophony of metropolitan life until Mark pulled into the parking lot of World's Best Electronics.

A chime jingled as we entered, causing a petite woman behind the counter to look up. She smiled, then went back to typing on a keyboard as Mark and I headed toward the big screen TVs along the far wall.

Mark spread his arms wide, each hand pointing at a different screen. "I'm stuck between the LG OLED and the Samsung."

Looking at both I really couldn't tell the difference. They both were crystal clear, as if looking through a freshly washed window. "I don't know. They both look good to me."

The woman from behind the counter approached, brushing a strand of long, black hair behind an ear. "May I help you with something?"

Mark looked down at her name tag, pointing at each television in turn. "Which one would you recommend, Amara?"

Amara smiled and her dark eyes sparkled with the reflection of the TVs. "I'd go for the Samsung."

"I think I'll accept your recommendation."

"Great. Meet me at the counter."

Amara disappeared into the back and I said, "See the way she was looking at you? Ask for her number."

"What? No. She was just trying to make the sale."

I shook my head. "I'm telling you, fam. Get her number."

She returned from the back with a big box on a cart. Mark paid, then I pushed the cart toward the door so he could get his mack on.

I'd been standing by the Tahoe for a few minutes when Mark walked out with a big smile on his face.

"See, that's what I'm talkin about!"

"You were right, you were right." He said. "We're going out Saturday."

I slapped him on the shoulder. "My man. Don't be too hard on her, though. Give her a chance."

We wrestled the TV into the back of the truck, then Mark took the cart back inside to say goodbye to Amara before we left.

8
Maia

Andrea put it down on the seafood boil, gumbo, and red beans and rice. Sire put a brisket on the smoker early in the morning, and I put together my famous four cheese macaroni, collard greens, and sweet potatoes. Desert came from a french bakery that Sire seemed to be very fond of.

Voices filtered in from the front room as Sire played host. If all of the noise was any indication, we'd have a full house for dinner, and as I looked around the kitchen at the amount of food we had prepared, I knew that we hadn't overdone it.

"I'm going to get dressed," I said to Andrea, then went upstairs to my room.

Andrea talked me into getting a sexy little gray and black, Fendi turtleneck mini and thigh-high black boots. As I laid the outfit on the bed I wasn't too sure about it. High-class fashionista wasn't how one would describe me, but I had to admit the dress was really cute. I put it on and looked in the mirror, noticing how all of my curves were on full display. This wasn't my regular jam, but…

Ya girl looked good.

Makeup and hair done, I went back downstairs, bypassing the kitchen and heading for the living room. People were everywhere, milling about with wine and weed in hand.

Sire walked up to me wearing a black african style shirt with an intricate silver design embroidered on the front, slack's, and Tom Ford loafers, and again I thought about how handsome he was, reminding me of T'Challa from Black Panther. He looked downright regal and I thought I understood where he got his name.

He leaned forward, handing me a glass of wine, and his fresh scent commandeered my senses.

"Damn, Maia. You look amazing."

Self-conscious, I issued a quiet, "Thank you," and took a sip of wine.

"Wow, this is good."

Sire smiled. "I'm not much of a drinker, so it all tastes bad to me. Do you smoke?"

I shook my head. "I tried it once, but it didn't do anything."

"It's a lot like wine with the varieties of scent and flavor profiles, but it's not for everyone I guess. Come on, let me introduce you to the gang."

He put his hand in the small of my back and guided me around the room. I thought it was a little intimate, but as I looked up he seemed not to notice. I recognized a few of the guys from his office, even the creepy guy, Squish, was in attendance.

The rest of the people were like a who's who when it came to ballers. The men's suits were tailored and expensive, and the women were slaying, their diamonds on full display like actresses at the Met Gala.

Suddenly, I felt overwhelmingly underdressed.

Andrea walked into the room and everyone's heads turned towards her. She was looking like a goddess wearing a gold dress with a high slit that complimented her golden skin, which was absolutely glowing.

Everyone filed into the dining room, sitting at a long, oak table and the few kids there went to a side room where they had their own set up.

Sire stood at the head of the table. "This has been a great year, so we definitely have much to be thankful about. I won't get too much into business, but everybody has a bonus coming. Today, we are thankful for all of our blessings. We're thankful for the people in our lives. And we give thanks to God for giving us this beautiful world with all of you beautiful people in it. We have come a long way and we have so much further to go. As we prepare for our journeys let us never forget where we came from so we can remain humble and bless others as we have been blessed. Now... I'm starving so let's eat."

Dinner was served buffet-style, and the kids got their plates before the adults got to dig in.

After dinner Sire took me by the hand and we walked to a side room. A slim, light-skinned guy with short locs was sitting on the arm of a leather chair by the door.

Sire nodded his head in my direction. "Menace, she's going to be riding with Will on that drop tonight."

Menace's head turned in my direction, looking at me up and down. "Who the fuck is she?"

"Dante's sister."

He snorted with laughter. "Get the fuck outta here."

Sire smiled. "I know, right."

"You sure about this?"

I spoke up. "I can handle myself."

"She got it," Sire said.

Menace rose from his seat. "Well, I guess you're up. Be ready in a couple hours. And I know you're not going on a run looking like that. You'll have every man in the city running behind the shipment."

Sire moved slightly in front of me and I could sense a change in his energy. "Stop flirting. You got business to handle."

Heading back to the kitchen to help with cleanup I left the two guys to it. I wasn't really looking forward to going on this run. I had never done anything like that before. Growing up, I saw the destruction that drugs caused every time I looked out the window. Crackheads and heroin addicts were a staple in my neighborhood, and not to be judgmental or anything, but they always seemed dirty and just out of it, the driving force in their lives the need to get their next fix. It had been hard on me when my brother decided to turn to the streets. I was always afraid that he would end up a zombie just like all the other addicts.

But at the same time I was feeling a rush of excitement. An energy coursed through my body, along with the butterfly wings of anxiety I felt in my stomach. It was an odd mixture of feelings that I wasn't used to and I tried to push it down and focus on the task at hand, but I was utterly unsuccessful.

After getting the food put up I tracked Chris down, but he was caught up in a video game with the other kids so I left him alone. He seemed to be in his element as they laughed and did the kid's version of trash talk. I was surprised by his ability to adapt to his new surroundings, but oddly enough, even I felt a certain sense of comfort in this house.

I changed clothes, throwing on a pair of jeans and a hoodie, which seemed appropriate for the job. Then I pulled my hair back into a ponytail and stepped into my Nike sneakers.

Ready to go.

A knock at the door startled me. "Come in."

Sire came in and stood by the door. "Ok. I see you're ready."

"Of course," I said, hoping that the quaver in my voice didn't betray my words.

"You're gonna be riding with Will. He's a'ight. But like all of these niggas, you can't let him see your fear. Move with confidence, like you belong. Like you've been doing this shit your entire life."

His eyes bored into mine and, again I felt as if he could see right through me. See right through the brave face I was trying to put on even though my insides were roiling like a turbulent sea.

I nodded. "I'm ready."

We headed out, ending up at a quaint little house with fresh white paint and a detached two car garage.

Ignoring the house altogether, Sire led me to a door on the side of the garage and entered. A nondescript car with its trunk open occupied one half of the garage, and the other side contained two rows of wooden pallets stacked waist high with plastic wrapped packages.

I stopped, frozen in place. "Is that..."

Sire smiled. "Yeah."

"Oh my gawd. How much..." My voice trailed off.

"Enough to make sure my team can eat."

This was some movie shit. Theoretically, I knew there were people moving weight like this, but to actually see it first hand was something else entirely. Sure, I've known d-boys my whole life as a black woman living in low income areas, but they were just trap boys serving addicts and playing with a few thousand here and there. This, on the other hand, was just ridiculous.

"Yeah, you jumped right off the porch and into the big leagues."

Mouth hanging open, I asked, "This is what my brother did?"

Sire simply nodded.

"What was he doing with all of his money?"

Shrugging his shoulders, Sire said, "Not my business. Hopefully he was saving it in case he ever got in a jam."

A red hot fury boiled my blood. Dante had been making tons of money while I was struggling my ass off and he couldn't even be consistent with his half of the bill and rent money. "Was he using?"

"If I knew about it he wouldn't have been working for me. I'm sorry lil mama, but I don't have the answers you're looking for."

Two men were busy arranging packages in the trunk of the car and when one of them looked up Sire waved him over.

"Will, this is Maia. She's gonna be riding with you tonight."

Will looked at me and nodded. "Yeah, I remember you from Patties." He turned his attention to Sire. "What about J Rock?"

"I got something else for him to do. Y'all ready to ride?"

Will stared at me as I stared back, not knowing what to say.

"We good," he said.

"The new routes are programmed into the gps. Any problems, just hit me."

Sire called for J Rock, leading him out of the door.

Will quietly shut the trunk. "I'm driving. You're gonna be my eyes. Anything look funny, let me know immediately. I mean anything. You get a weird feeling about some shit, speak up. Got me?"

"Yes."

"A'ight. We got three deliveries to make. It's gonna seem like we're driving around in circles, and we really kinda are. It's like the spy movies, right. Run around in circles in case we have a tail. That way we flush them out. Don't worry, though. I've never actually had any problems, but we still gotta do it just to be on point. Got me?"

I nodded as I opened the passenger side door and ducked down into the seat.

Behind the wheel, Will said, "There's a gun in the glove box, one in the door, and the tech is under your seat. Same for my side, except for the glove box. Got me? You know how to shoot, right?"

I had never shot a gun before, but I'd seen tons of action movies and thought I understood the concept. "Point it and pull the trigger?"

"You got it. Let's roll. Remember, keep your eyes open."

That wasn't something he'd have to worry about. I was already looking around, using the mirrors and we hadn't even left the garage.

Traffic was light as the gps guided us along and I guessed that the few people who were out were heading towards one Black Friday sale or another. Leaving the residential areas behind, we jumped on the highway for a couple miles before exiting back onto the streets.

As we pulled to a stop at a light I noticed a blue Chevy behind us that I thought I'd seen on the highway. "See that Chevy a couple cars back? I'm not sure, but I think I saw them on the highway, too."

Will's eyes went to the rearview. "Think it's the laws?"

I shook my head. "Not sure, but I don't think so. Car's too old."

"A'ight. Keep your eyes on them. We're gonna stick to the plan until we know for sure. Got me?"

After a couple turns along the route I noticed that the blue Chevy was still behind us, three cars back. Pulling out my cell I called Sire.

"What's up? Y'all good?"

I said, "Somebody's following us in a blue Chevy."

"Is it the police? Feds?" he asked.

I stole another glance behind us. "I don't think so."

"Where y'all at?"

Looking at the gps, I told him.

"Look, y'all are gonna hit a remote straightaway in about five minutes. Me and J Rock ain't too far away. We'll meet you there and run interference." Sire hung up.

Will asked, "What he say?"

"He's going to meet us at the straightaway."

"A'ight, once we hit it grab the tech from under your seat and stay ready."

Reaching under my seat I felt the cold metal and my heart jumped into overdrive. What the fuck had I gotten myself into? Preparing for a gunfight on the road? Seriously?

My bed had already been made and I was securely tucked in. Nothing I could do about it now but do my best to make sure I made it home safely.

And alive.

The gps showed the straightaway coming up after the next turn. I cradled the tech in my arms, one hand around the grip and the other holding the magazine protruding from beneath the barrel.

We turned into the straightaway and the Chevy followed suit. We had the road to ourselves being the only two cars for as far as the eye could see. And I could see pretty far. It made sense that Sire would select this road as part of the new route. No one would be able to sneak up on us.

The isolation made me nervous, though. This would be the perfect place for violence to erupt and no one would be the wiser.

Where was Sire? He needed to hurry up.

Ahead, I could make out a cross street, although it was still far away. Checking the mirror, I saw that the Chevy was gaining on us.

Where the fuck was Sire?

As we approached the cross street I noticed a car sitting at the stop sign waiting for us to pass since we had the right of way. Surely the car behind us wouldn't make a move with a witness sitting there. I relaxed the death hold I had on my gun. Just a little.

Looking back again I saw a speck of movement, but it was so far away that I couldn't even be certain that it *was* a car.

The vehicle at the stop sign pulled into the middle of the road just as we were approaching and I thought to myself how stupid they were to wait all this time just to pull out right when we got there, but Will's voice cut into my thoughts.

"Heads up! They're blocking us in," he said as he hit the brakes and dropped his hand into the pocket of the door.

Throwing our car into reverse, Will tried to back up and swerve around the Chevy, but the driver cut the where to the side, causing the car to skid to a stop sideways across the street and effectively blocking our escape.

Will said, "Take the car in front. I'll take the car in back. Spray them muthafuckas down. Don't even give them a chance to shoot back."

The driver's door on the car in front opened and I just pulled the trigger. The windshield spider-webbed around the three holes left from my single pull off the trigger, ruining my visibility. The gun damn near flew from my hands with the force of the discharge and I released a brief scream.

The noise was something I hadn't expected. I couldn't hear shit, not even my own scream. I was deaf, except for the ever present ringing in my ears. It was a little disorienting and the cracked windshield didn't help.

Looking to my left I saw that Will's door was open and he was missing, so taking his cue, I opened my own door and stepped out. As soon as my feet hit the asphalt I tightened my grip with all the strength I had and repeatedly pulled that trigger until I no longer felt the forceful jerk of my weapon.

Noticing that I was no longer firing, the driver opened his door, fully exposing himself and our eyes met. He hesitated a second, but it was enough time for me to dive head first into the tall grass on the side of the road.

I lay in the grass for what seemed like forever, waiting for someone to come put a bullet in my head while praying, praying, praying that no one did. In all actuality it was only maybe a minute or two, but time was distorted as adrenaline and fear clenched my gut.

The edges of a figure came into view, walking directly towards me. This was it. After a lifetime of playing it safe I was on my way to meet my maker after my first walk on the wild side. I felt a tickling on my cheek as tears began falling from my eyes. I didn't want to die, but what could I do? There was nowhere to run, nowhere to hide; the land was flat and bare for as far as the eye could see.

A hand touched my shoulder and I realized that my eyes were closed. Opening my eyes I saw Sire kneeling next to me and I jumped up, throwing my arms around his neck.

Sire stood, pulling me up with him and I felt rather than heard him grunt against my cheek. I took a step back and noticed an ever widening red stain spreading across the front of his shirt.

"You're hurt," I said.

He mouthed, "I'm fine," and led me back onto the street.

The car that blocked us from the front was gone, but the tail car was still there and looked like a pegboard with all of the holes in it.

A step later Sire fell to a knee and I dropped to mine.

"Get in the car!" he screamed at me. "I'm fine, but I need you to drive."

Hardheaded, I stayed with him until he regained his feet, then I rushed around to the driver's side and climbed in as Sire fell into the passenger seat.

"Turn around and follow J Rock," he said weakly.

"You need a doctor."

"No," was his only reply.

After getting the car turned around I smashed into the side of the trunk of the blue Chevy and pushed it out of the way, then followed J Rock.

"Where are we going?" I asked Sire, but only heard silence in response.

"Sire! Sire!"

Nothing.

9
Sire

I woke up, opening my eyes to the bright light filtering through the window, and immediately closed them against the glare. My room had both north and east facing windows, and the light told me that it was morning.

Eyes closed, I took a mental inventory of myself, wiggling fingers and toes, flexing muscles. Everything seemed to be working.

I tried to open my eyes again, just enough to let a sliver of light in. The TV hanging on the wall directly in front of me silently displayed some game show, a lucky contestant jumping up and down in celebration.

My head hurt. My mouth felt like I'd been gargling with sand for an entire year. And just then I got the overwhelming urge to take a leak.

I tried to sit up and swing my legs over the side of the bed, but that was when the pain hit. Felt like something was clawing its way out of both my back and my chest. Clenching my teeth against the pain I tried to relax and take a deep breath, but I ended up just sitting there for a minute until the wave of dizziness and nausea passed.

Wearing nothing but boxer briefs I shuffled my way toward the bathroom. Felt the cold of the tile against my feet as I crossed the threshold. My body was stiff and I wondered how long I had been unconscious.

After relieving myself I stopped in front of the mirror, hands on the counter and looked at the neat bandage covering the right side of my chest. I had to look, had to see what damage had been done to my body, so I peeled the bandage back, trying not to scream as it came off.

Fuck.

At least the wound was already starting to heal. Which made me wonder how long I had been out.

After taking a shower and brushing my teeth I stepped back onto the soft carpet of my bedroom floor and was met by a beautiful surprise. Maia sat on the edge of my bed with a big, cheesy grin on her face.

"How long was I out?"

"About a week," she said. "For a while I was worried you had lost too much blood, but you're obviously a fighter."

I pointed to my wound. "Who's been taking care of this?"

"Me."

"You did a good job. No infection or anything. Thanks."

"I've been working in the medical field since I was eighteen. Plus, it was a clean shot. You were lucky. I need to bandage it up again, though."

Sitting next to her on the bed I was suddenly aware that I was completely naked. Until she began poking and prodding around my wound.

"Does that hurt?" she asked.

I gritted my teeth. "Yes."

"Scale of one to ten?"

"Shit, with you poking it, ten." I took a breath. "I've dealt with worse though."

She taped a fresh piece of gauze to my chest. "You'll live." With her hand on my bare thigh, she stood and started walking to the door. "Get dressed. I'll be back with some food."

Doing as bid, I threw on a fresh pair of boxer briefs and sweats, then headed for the door just as Maia cane in with a bowl of stew on a small tray.

She set the tray on my bed. "Sit down and eat. You need to save your strength."

"What I need to do is figure out who fucking shot me."

Just as I was raising the spoon to my mouth, Maia started shifting her weight from foot to foot, then she said, "Ummm..."

"What? If Thanksgiving was any indication I know you can cook. It can't be that bad."

"It's not that. I know one of the guys. I know who did it."

Dropping the spoon back into the bowl before I could even take a bite I said, "The fuck you mean you know who did it?"

"One of the guys..." she stammered. "The guy I was shooting at. After my gun went empty he stepped out of the car and I saw him. Looked right into his eyes. I know it's him."

"Who are you talking about? What the fuck do you mean you know it's him? You need to stop talking in circles and tell me what the fuck is going on here."

"This little dude, Daygo. I went to middle school with him and he's always had a crush on me. Everytime he sees me he tries to talk to me. It's definitely him."

I stood, faced Maia. "You emptied your gun into his car, didn't hit shit. Now you tell me you know this nigga? What the fuck am I supposed to make of this? You set me up? Huh? Did you fucking set me up?"

"No, Sire! Stop it! You're acting crazy."

"Crazy? Nah, I'ma tell you what's crazy. First, your brother gets busted with my shit. Then you insist on coming to stay with me. And now you tell me you know the niggas who shot and tried to rob me? Come on, now. Miss me with the crazy shit because all this crazy ass shit seems to be revolving around you."

She looked at the floor. "I don't know what you want me to say."

"Tell me the fucking truth!" I yelled.

"I am telling you the truth. I haven't lied to you once. Not one time since I've known you."

I turned and slammed my fist into the wall. "What the fuck Maia? Where is Andrea? Is she here?" Opening the bedroom door, I called for her. "Andrea!"

"She's not here. Look, Sire. You need to just calm down and think about this for a minute. I've been right here by your side, taking care of you since the moment you got shot. I'm new. I don't know anything about what's going on around here. There's no way I could have set any of this up. I don't know any of the routes, nothing. Think about it, Sire! You're not stupid at all. Just calm down and think about it."

I spread my arms. "Why? Why would you do all of this for me?"

"I don't know. I just... I don't know, why not?"

Logic was starting to work its way back into my brain and I really thought about it. She was right. How could she have known any of the information she would have needed to know in order to pull this off? Just wasn't possible.

I sat back down on the bed and grabbed the bowl of stew, keeping my eyes on Maia the entire time. Took a bite and was transported back to my childhood, sitting at my grandmother's table and eating her stew on a cold winter day.

"This is good."

I had never felt this hungry in my life and I ate the entire bowl without saying another word.

"I'm sorry, Maia. I'm just not understanding what's going on. Nothing is making sense. Tell me about him. What's the deal with this guy? I gotta figure out how he was able to set this up and hit us in the middle of a route that had never been run before."

She moved the tray and sat next to me on the bed. "There's nothing special about him. Just a regular guy. Now that you say that, it's hard for me to imagine him setting this all up by himself, but I really don't know him that well."

Taking her hand in mine, I said, "Thank you. I really mean it. I might not have made it without you and that means a lot. Hell, that means everything. Have we heard any news on your brother?"

"He had a hearing on Monday. Judge denied him bail."

"Anything I can do just let me know."

Giving my hand a squeeze, Maia took the tray and headed out the door, closing it behind her.

10
Andrea

I had been sitting in a rental, down the street from these lil niggas' spot for a couple hours before I saw anyone show up. He was a stocky, dark skinned guy with thick locs that looked like they were about a year old.

Once Sire told me that Maia knew who one of the guys was it was short work finding where they hung out. Now I watched him cross through the front yard and enter the front door.

I got out of the car wearing dark gray sweats, Air Max's and a hoodie, and walked up the driveway and along the walkway to the same door.

I knocked.

It took a minute before I heard the lock disengage. Must have been trying to check me out and determine if I was a threat.

I may not have looked like it, but I definitely was.

After he opened the door a crack I said, "Hi. My car broke down just over there..." I pointed.

He looked.

The sound of the gunshot was barely audible, being that of a small caliber .22, but it's impact was immediate. The bullet ripped through the flesh of his leg, tearing muscle necessary to hold his weight. He fell backwards, into the house and I stepped in as well, closing the door behind me.

"Bitch! What the fuck? You fucking shot me!"

I put a foot on his leg wound. "Shut the fuck up lil bitch as nigga. I'll ask the questions. You and your homies tried to rob us, right?"

"Fuck you," he said through gritted teeth. "I don't know nothing."

I smiled. "You obviously don't know who I am. That's fine. You'll learn fast and you'll be begging me to tell everything you know."

Stepping over him after a quick pat-down in search of weapons, I went looking for the kitchen. After finding what I was looking for, I came back to him struggling up to his one good leg. Easily pushing his weight toward his damaged leg was enough to put him back on the floor.

I stood over him with the serrated steak knife I had snatched from the kitchen to his throat and he looked up at me with wide eyes. That wasn't enough. He was bigger than I and could probably still overpower me even with his bum leg. I needed to break him, strike the fear of God into him in order to get what I wanted and make it out of here unscathed.

Tracing the sharp edge of the knife along his collar bone, I drug it down the center of his chest and stomach, over his belly button, until I reached his belt. Unbuckling his pants with my free hand, I exposed his shriveled penis and let the tip of the knife kiss the tip of his dick.

"No! Please don't. Please! Fuck, you're crazy. Please don't do it. Please!"

"Ain't nothing worse than a sexy nigga with a lil dick. A bitch be thinking like, I know this nigga bout to work my ass out. Foreplay be good. I bet you can eat the shit outta some pussy, can't you? Have a bitch all wet and shit. Ready to get dicked down. Then you pull out some shit like this." I tapped the cold, steel blade against the length of it.

He was frozen with terror, his only movements the tremor that caused his entire body to shake like a mini seizure.

"Are you the one who shot Sire?"

His head shook. "No! No, it was Daygo."

"How did y'all set it up? Who told you about our routes?"

His words came out in a stutter. "We've been watching the stash house ever since y'all switched up your movements."

"Where's Daygo? When is he supposed to show up?"

"He's not."

I let the sharp edge trace the length of his penis.

"I'm telling the truth! Please don't. None of us are supposed to be here. I just needed to get my weed real quick. That's all I was doing. I just came to get some weed. We're supposed to be laying low until the heat passes. I just needed some weed."

"Last chance," I said. "Where can I find him?"

Raising his hands in a gesture of honesty, he said, "I swear to you, I don't know."

Rising to my feet I put the knife in the pocket of my hoodie. "Pull your pants up."

Quickly, he grabbed his pants and buckled his belt through gritted teeth. Once he was proper his eyes moved up to the .22 I held, but he never had a chance to say anything. The bullet entered his forehead just above his nose and his head dropped to the floor with a hollow thump.

11
Sire

Dodging around obstacles, the car sped along in pursuit of the car ahead, which happened to be driven by what appeared to be a rabbit. Playing whatever racing game that was on the TV screen, Maia and Chris giggled as she kept telling him how she was catching up.

I stood in the doorway for a moment, watching aunt and nephew as the distraction of the game filled their attention, pushing out any thought of the many stressors our world had to throw at us. It was good seeing them laugh - seeing her laugh. She had been going beyond the call of duty when it came to helping me recover and deserved all of the laughter she could stand.

I cleared my throat and Maia looked up, concern washing over her features.

"You should be in bed, resting."

I shrugged my shoulders. "I've been in bed for the past three weeks. I'm done laying around. Come on. I want to take y'all somewhere."

Maia stood. "No. You need to get back upstairs. Trying to act like you've been just laying around, knowing you've been getting up at the crack of dawn to go hide out in that shipping container you got out back."

Laughter rose from my gut. "It's like we're married already. Next thing I know you'll be telling me to stop eating burgers."

"You're not funny. Where do you think you're going anyway?" she asked, taking in the fact that I was fully dressed and wearing a jacket.

"I have a tradition that I haven't missed since I was a kid, and this won't be the first year. Fuck being shot. Come on, let's go."

After grabbing their jackets we jumped in my Camaro and set out just as the sun dipped below the horizon. The park was crowded and we ended up having to park down the street, but it was a short walk and we soon passed through the entrance.

A short path opened up and Chris's eyes widened in awe. The park had been turned into a winter festival of lights. A group of snowmen greeted us, and as we moved deeper inside we could see that everything had been decorated.

Roaming carolers approached and we sang along with them, getting into the spirit of the season before moving on to a life size Santa, his sleigh being pulled by a team of reindeer.

Next, we walked past the gates of a castle, its battlements draped with colorful lights, but it was the train across from the castle that drew Chris's attention.

As we stood in line, Maia said, "This place is amazing and I never even knew it was here."

My eyes went to Chris. "My aunt used to bring me every year. If it wasn't for her, I don't think I would have ever known it was here either."

Reaching the front of the line, Chris boarded the small train while Maia and I took a seat on a bench beneath the soft glow of the lights hanging from the roof of the arcade.

Maia put a hand on my forearm. "So, you were raised by your aunt?"

"Not really. It was all of the women in my family. My mom, grandma, aunts. They all kind of shared all of us kids. We were always over each other's homes. I guess they did what they had to do since none of our fathers were around."

Maia made a muscle. "That's just what we do."

I smiled. "True, black women are as strong as it gets, but stop it lil mama. You don't have no muscles."

"What?" she exclaimed. "You just can't see them. My strength comes from my soul."

I felt that shit. "Now that I'm older I look back and I can notice all of the times they had to be strong, and we were just needy little things. Didn't have a clue."

Maia's eyes dug into mine as she asked, "Is that why you don't have kids? I mean, all these guys have a baby mama or two."

"A family is responsibility, and as long as I'm in these streets I could be ripped from that at any moment. I don't want to do mine like that."

I had even considered having a vasectomy and just reversing it whenever I got ready to settle down, but I couldn't get comfortable with the idea of someone playing around down there with a razor sharp knife. Since that option was off the table I made sure to play it safe and strap up whenever I went there with a woman.

Which wasn't that often. I'd always been picky. The girls I grew up around were just as raw as the niggas and you couldn't trust them as far as you could throw them. Getting caught up with the wrong one could have grave consequences on your life and I didn't have time for that shit.

So I was careful with whom I shared my bed. True, my sex life wasn't quite what I wished, but that was by design.

Chris emerged from the train, going on about all of the lights he'd seen, and we made our way to the restaurant at the far end of the park. The wait for a table was short and we were seated and given menus within minutes.

The food arrived and we ate. I was starving. That had been the norm since I'd gotten shot and I figured that my body had a lot of repairs to make and needed all of the energy it could get.

After dinner we headed home and Chris was already passed out by the time we got there. After carrying him up the stairs and getting him in bed I sought out Maia, finding her curled up on the couch in the living room with her feet tucked under her and a book in hand.

"Don't mean to interrupt, but I have something I'd like to show you."

She closed the book and unfolded her body. "You're not interrupting. Thanks for getting Chris in bed."

I led Maia through the kitchen and out into the backyard where we stood in front of the storage container. "This is what I've been doing when I come out here to 'hide' in the mornings."

Opening the door, I stepped inside, turning the light on as she came in behind. She looked around, and I could tell that she wasn't quite sure what she was looking at.

"It's a grow room. I'm building it for my cousin."

"You did all of this? Yourself?" she asked.

"Yeah. And the best thing about it is it runs off solar power. Well, technically it's running off of batteries right now. But the sun charges the batteries."

She walked along the container's interior, looking at all of the equipment. "You ever thought about selling these? I could see the commercial now. 'Grow your green with green en-er-gy.' Or something like that."

I laughed like that was the funniest thing I'd ever heard. She was funny, smart, caring. Easy to be around. I didn't feel the need to have to stay on my toes every second. It was as if I'd known her my entire life.

I had heard people talk about that - meeting someone you felt like you've always known. Never understood how that was possible, and still don't, even though I was standing here experiencing it first hand. It was like she was the old friend that I'd been missing my entire life.

"You are full of surprises, Mr. Sire."

"You're beautiful." The compliment was one that just happened, in conflict with my intentions. Of course she was beautiful, but I hadn't meant to say it.

Just like the kiss that happened next. Didn't plan it, didn't even think about it. One moment I was chiding myself about the compliment that shouldn't have been, and the next moment I was watching my own body as it was inexorably drawn into her's, my lips making contact with her full lips that were so soft I could have curled up and slept for a year.

Eyes closed, Maia wrapped her arms around my neck and I pulled her tight into my embrace.

My body reacted to her, and again, it was unintentional. I could feel the press of my dick against my pants and I didn't want to be poking her all in the stomach, so I broke the embrace, going against everything my heart and physical wanted to do.

"I'm sorry," I said, lost in her eyes. "I shouldn't have done that."

Taking my face in her hands, Maia pulled my lips back down to her's, and my mind said, *fuck it*.

I wanted this woman, more than I'd ever wanted anyone. Her curves felt perfect in my hands. Her kiss was passionate, hungry. The scent of her hair filled my nostrils, transporting me to an island paradise where we were the only inhabitants, free to make love as we lazed in the warm, crystal clear water.

The door to the shipping container clanged, causing both of us to jump and look up as if we were hormone imbalanced teenagers who had just got caught making out by the principal.

Chris stood at the entrance, wide eyes on Maia as he asked, "Aunty Maia, is he your boyfriend?"

12
Daygo

The perfect ass grinding against me should have had me on hard. It would have any other time, but no matter how hard she twerked, I felt like I was stuffing dollars in her g-string for no reason.

Oh well, I thought as I took another shot of tequila.

Then another.

Stuffing a few more dollars in her g-string, I pushed her out of the way and made my way out of the strip club. There was a liquor store about a block away and I stumbled my way there, following the siren's call in an effort to feel nothing.

The store's selection was overwhelming so I just grabbed a big bottle of something strong and paid a cashier that I couldn't remember even though I had just walked out of the store.

Those bitch ass niggas got Byrd in our own spot. On our home turf. What the fuck was he even doing there? He knew better. Everybody was supposed to hide out for a while, lay low. Stay the fuck outta dodge.

I knew they would be coming for us. Especially since that bitch Maia had seen my face. And what the fuck was she doing on a drop? That's what was the most confusing thing of all. Maia was square, had never been involved in street shit. That was part of what drove me crazy when it came to her; she was different than all these other bitches.

Apparently not. Saw it with my own eyes. And she nearly killed me.

There has to be more to it. That's just not her.

Byrd is dead, right?

Maia had to give him up. That's the only way they would have found the spot.

She was with them, part of the Hit Team now.

I can't win for losing. The lick went to shit, Maia done chose up with these bitch ass niggas, and now Byrd is gone.

Opening the brown bag, I popped the top on the alcohol and took a sip. Shit burned as it went down.

Good.

A bus pulled to a stop a few yards ahead of me and I made it just as the last person in line stepped on. After paying the toll I shuffled to the back and took a seat. The phone buzzed in my pocket, but I didn't care. Fuck that phone. It could ring until the sky fell, for all I cared.

My stop approached so I stood and exited the bus. Standing on the sidewalk, I took another long drink, then walked past a doughnut shop thinking how I should stop and get something to eat, but I wasn't hungry.

The street was dark. Moonlight that was periodically obscured by clouds provided the only illumination, but it was enough to make out the outline of a church's spires a couple hundred yards away.

My foot caught on a loose rock and I stumbled. After finding my equilibrium I kicked at the rock in frustration, missing it the first two times and finally connecting with the third. The rock launched into the air, landing against the waxed and polished door of a Mustang, leaving a small dent and scratch.

That's what they get.

The homes lining the street gave way to a dense area of trees and foliage that completely blocked the moonlight as I crossed the eerily dark stretch. Made me think of all the scary stories my older cousins would tell me when I was a kid, trying to scare me. It was a good thing that I didn't believe in ghosts, else I would have ran through at full speed.

Moonlight revealed itself again as I stepped from the dense overhang and stood before a tall structure of gray stone.

Walking around the church, its gray spire towering above, I crossed its grounds and headed for the cemetery behind. After finding the headstone I was looking for, I knelt. The earth was still loose from being freshly disturbed. Byrd's funeral was only yesterday.

Opening the bottle, I poured a little over Byrd's grave then raised it to my lips and took a long drink. More like a few gulps.

"I'ma make this right, fam. This wasn't supposed to be you. Not you. Why'd you go back? I told you not to go back to the spot until the heat died down. What were you thinking? Fuck, man."

I took another drink, but my body was numbing to its burn, so I hit it harder.

"I'ma get em, Byrd. You have my word on that. I'm gonna have your back just like you always had mine. Like that time back in ninth grade when I got into it with the Mexicans. It was four to one. They was going to beat my ass, and they really should have. I sold that fool, Guillermo some straight oregano." I laughed at the memory.

"I don't know what I was thinking trying to sell some Mexicans some fake weed. But out of nowhere, here your ass come running down the hallway. They ain't want no smoke then.

"Or, how about that time I grabbed Maia's booty, but when she turned around she saw you. Man, she was tripping. You never gave me up, though. That's real nigga shit. You was a real nigga, Byrd. A real nigga."

And Maia had never been with the bullshit. Never. Something wasn't right. There's no way she would be moving product. That nigga Sire must have something on her.

But, what? She was too clean. There was nothing to hold over her head and I refused to believe that she had been living this secret life.

Whatever was going on, I had to figure it out and save her.

"I'm sorry, Byrd. I should have never gotten you caught up in this shit. But you should have stayed away from the spot. I'ma take that nigga Sire down. Believe that."

Rising to my feet, I took another long drink from the bottle then poured the rest onto Byrd's grave. "Rest in heaven, fam. Love."

Sire 2 will be released on January 26, 2021.
Get your copy now and follow this wild story to
its shocking end.

Or, you can check out my must read thriller,
Certain Reprisal.

Thanks for reading and taking these trips
with me and the characters I create. We
appreciate the love!

And don't forget to leave an honest review.